I0604138

life on other moons

life on other moons

Roger Market

For more information:
www.roger.market
hello@roger.market

ISBN (paperback): 978-0-9892466-2-0

First e-book edition: November 2014
First print editions (paperback and handmade): May 2013

"King Henry on a Porch Swing" first appeared in *Welter* magazine in May 2013.

Designed, typeset, and published in the United States.

Book design: Roger Market
Photography: Danielle Crawford

for Justin
  my pocket rocket on this journey.

Acknowledgments

This book would not be in your hands without the knowledge, inspiration, love, and support of a lot of people. I couldn't possibly list everyone who's guided me or put up with me or, in some way, shined a light on me in my journey to make *Life on Other Moons* a possibility, but I'll hit the highlights.

First, I need to thank Justin Sosebee for being patient throughout this process and for listening to me bitch about apostrophes and production schedules. I love you, Justin.

Next, I want to thank Karen Brehmer for being one of my most loyal supporters. I don't always deserve it.

Then there's my family. Thanks to my mom, Tammy Smith; my dad, Roger E. Market; my sisters, Krista and Kayla Market; and everyone on the extended family tree…which could fill a book by itself. And especially to the most voracious reader in the family—and perhaps my most fervent, hopeful supporter: thank you, Aunt Terri.

While in Baltimore, I've met a lot of great people. Fantastic writers and teachers whom I'm proud to call friends and mentors. So here's to them, but especially to Lori Miller, Eli Dillard, Danielle Crawford, Christine Lincoln, Christina Lengyel, Emily Lee, Timmy Reed, Jessica Jonas, Megan Stolz, Kimberley Lynne, Jane Delury, Steve Matanle, Kendra Kopelke, Marion Winik, Jenny O'Grady, Pantea Tofangchi, Theresa Segreti, Peter Toran, and Gregg Wilhelm. You all taught me what a book or story is and what it can be.

Thank you to some other people who have supported me as a writer, artist, and person: Amanda Oldham, Michael Lunsford, Sande Bemis, Susie Runyon (you'll always be Mrs. Runyon to me), Jamie Britton, Robin Pruett, Stephanie Pezan, Hélène Huet, Toby Herzog, Warren and Julia Rosenberg, Thomas Campbell, Kristen Wilkins, Arielle Krasner, Kim Sullivan and the team at Words & Numbers, and Annie and Steve Larkin.

Finally, to Joy Castro: brilliant college professor, author, mother, woman. Your encouragement, wisdom, and grace have touched every page of this book. You've helped make me the writer and editor I am today. Thank you for always pushing me and believing in me.

Contents

Stopping to Talk to Porch Lights When the Moon Is Not Enough

As far as I knew, my mother was the last woman alive on Earth the day her heart stopped beating in the produce section and she plunged face-first into the romaine. I was eight at the time, and my best friend, Matthew, was with us. In the ten years after that, I didn't see a single woman, and neither did any other man I knew. We were in a lonely new world. But in that world, there was Matthew, and he had a way of making things better. We stuck together, even in college.

One night, when I was a freshman, I was sitting on the lawn of the Sigma Chi house, smoking, when the moon, the last great symbol of femininity, broke in half like a walnut cracking. A single egg-shaped object hurtled from the moon toward Earth and burst into flames when it hit the atmosphere. The two moon chunks floated there among the stars, and I watched them dance around each other for what seemed like hours. I wondered about the egg-shaped fireball that had fallen.

The next day, there were theories about the moon's split. I walked around campus and heard them all. For instance, the religious men of campus, who held prayer circles on the mall, thought maybe the world was coming to an end and the extinction of women had been the first step. Others thought it had something to do with the weight of Russian salmon or the way men drove with reckless abandon in the new world; the more red lights we ran, the closer the moon came to cracking under the pressure of universal chaos. Or maybe it was alien warfare.

Matthew was a sophomore and a Lambda Chi whose first love was science, and he had his own opinions about what had happened to the moon. I never understood them, and usually, he would realize this early on and stop talking over my head. He would laugh.

"Sorry," he would say. "Did I upset your soft little English major noggin?"

Then he would reach both arms out and pull me toward him in one smooth motion, reeling me in, like a master fisherman.

"Beard burn!" he would say at the top of his lungs.

And within seconds, I would feel the rough sting of his five o'clock shadow as he buried his face in my neck and shook his head back and forth, occasionally brushing his lips against my skin. He would laugh at me as I pretended to pull away. In those moments, I never knew what he was thinking, but for myself, I was hoping: each time, wanting his lips to stay still on contact and maybe suck in a little bit so that a tiny part of me would go inside him, just for a second. It would be almost like a kiss, which I'd never had, not even when there were women.

In the days and weeks after the moon became the moons, I saw a new category of men arise both on and off campus. I knew some of these men personally, and I knew that they still had hope for the world when the women started dying, or at least for men. Some had even gone off to search for women once it seemed clear that we were alone, just to prove we weren't and the human race was safe, but they had so far returned empty-handed. They were psychologically fragile afterward.

One night, I went to the window at the entrance to Sigma Chi and looked out. I was alone. While I gazed out the window, a silver-haired man who I knew to be a religion professor at the college came walking down the avenue, wearing only a plain white T-shirt, occasionally making a stop at a house with its porch light on. He looked like a drunken frat boy. Or, rather, a drunken former frat boy trying to relive his glory days. I couldn't hear him, but I knew he was speaking to the lights. He spoke calmly, tenderly, as if the lights were people he cared about, maybe women. Maybe his dead mother or sister. I watched the all-but-naked man as he chatted up the avenue's porch lights until he drifted out of sight.

A few weeks after I saw the first of these men, Matthew and I went out drinking at a popular hole-in-the-wall bar. It was cheap, and it was close. All the men from the college went there. I'd heard stories of this place in its heyday, when young men would line up at the bar to talk to a crew of female bartenders with eccentric nicknames. Barkin' Larkin apparently had the loudest voice of them all and could bellow out an audible what-can-I-get-ya even over the loudest music. As if she'd been born and raised in a bar. She had black hair with blue streaks, and she was sweet unless you crossed her or got in a fight. She was a legend. I heard she died of a brain aneurysm.

Now the bar was staffed with thirty-something men with boring brown hair and common names like Larry and Joe and Larry Joe. Tonight, it was Larry Joe.

"A vodka tonic!" I said.

"What?"

"A *vodka tonic*!" I said even louder.

Matthew got himself a sour, and we sat in the corner and drank and talked about the upcoming statistics final and then about the moons. He theorized that global warming had made the oceans rise, which wreaked havoc on the tides, and ultimately that was what had cracked the moon. That was the part I understood. When he started writing equations on napkins, I put my hand on his. He dropped the pen and looked at me.

"Sorry," he said, "got carried away again."

"It's okay, I just don't understand it. I can barely get through stats as it is. And only with your help."

I winked. He pulled my hand up to his chin and rubbed the two together.

"You're adorable," Matthew said as he let go.

"I know."

"I love you, man. For serious."

This took several seconds to process. He'd never said anything this affectionate to me before, though it was clear he was comfortable getting close physically.

"Do you mean that?" I said.

"I said *for serious*, didn't I?"

Now he winked.

"How could I not?" he said. "Haven't we always been best friends, like forever?"

I nodded as I realized what he meant. We were friends, and that is how things would remain. We would die virgins, probably the same day, probably together but still needlessly alone. Now the question was how. Would whatever had taken the women come back for us one day? Was the moon's split the first step indeed? Suddenly I felt sick. I was about to excuse myself when three frat boys rushed into the bar, knocking a man over at the door.

"Dudes, check this out," one of them said. "There's a fucking queen on the avenue!"

There was a stampede as most of the men in the bar rushed outside, bottlenecking at the door, some trading punches. Matthew and I were the last to move toward the door, and we did so quietly by comparison. Larry Joe stayed behind, cleaning beer off the bar with a dirty white rag, talking to another young man who couldn't be bothered by a queen.

The rest of us were curious.

On the avenue was a woman in a white robe with a crown on her head. She stood in the middle of the road, and as Matthew and I got closer, the students who'd left before us were already surrounding her and staring. Men from the town walked toward the crowd as well, some of them with blank expressions on their faces, stopping to talk to porch lights along the way. It was then that I noticed some of the students, too, were talking to porch lights. I'd never seen so many of these porch light men before in one place.

"Look," I said. "So many of them. They're nuts."

We stopped walking, and one of the porch light men pointed at the queen. "Girl," he said. He rubbed his crotch.

"Do you think this will happen to all of us?" I said, looking at Matthew.

"Don't know," he said.

"What do you mean you don't know? You always have an opinion."

"This time I'm speechless."

He laughed, and I knew he was nervous.

"Just as long as you don't start talking to porch lights," I said. "I can't have you turning on me. I'd be lost."

He shook his head. "I'd never turn on you. Not for a woman, if that's what's going on."

We looked at the crowd once more and saw it in the midst of change. Some men walked from house to house, talking to porch lights, perhaps gearing up to go meet the queen. Others just crowded around her and looked. She stood there in her robe of white. She swayed on the spot like the moon dancing with itself.

"You won't be able to help it, though," I said. "Look at them, they're lonely."

"I think whatever affected them can't get us. We have each other. We always will."

"But am I enough?"

He put his arms out and reeled me in once more, but this time, it was his lips that he pressed against my neck. There was no beard burn. He looked up.

"Even if you were broken like the moon, you'd be more than enough," he said. "I love every little piece of you, and I mean that."

I hugged him tighter. "I've wanted to kiss you since I was six," I said.

"I know," he said. "Do it."

So I did, and suddenly the queen didn't matter very much. And neither did the moon.

Paterfamilias

It was very early on a Sunday, still somewhat dark out, and he was alone on the tiny island of a dirty Alabama river. Already, he had managed to clean up the brush from the storm the night before, freeing a trapped squirrel in the process. It had thanked him with a nudge from its nose. It had called him "master," and he had crowned himself king of the river island and of the constituents of the surrounding forest.

But he had a gun with him, and on his clothes, he wore the colors and patterns and smells of nature. There was deer pee on his shoes and, though he'd tried to avoid it, even in his hair. This was the hunting protocol he had learned as a young man. He had come here today not out of the kindness of his heart but out of a need to provide for his family.

Not long after his enthronement, he saw the deer enter the clearing. He lifted his gun, lined up the crosshairs, fired. The animals went wild. Around him, blackbirds cawed in anger; trout flipped their tails at him; other animals began to flee. The squirrel that had been so gracious was now long gone.

Now the deer lay dead at his feet, ready to be dressed. He held the knife in his hand. He was sedulous and unrelenting. He worked alone, sitting in the deer's pluck and pondering the nature of life and the question of God and why he had really come to the river island today—and what was in store for him in the wilds of Vietnam.

He thought of his father, who had taught him not only how to kill and field dress almost anything under the sun but also that it was necessary. Such knowledge had been passed down from father to son for generations. By now, this son was a pro with the equivalent forethought and practice of a hundred other men in the McKee lineage running through his mind, his veins, his entire being. Hunting was what a man was supposed to do in the McKee household. In fact, it seemed everything he did lately was "what a man should do." He was shipping out soon to serve his country, to hunt down the Viet Cong. To protect his family. Although he was proud of his service, he knew there was a chance it could deprive the next generation. Acting as a man, as the paterfamilias of his family, had always felt natural to him. He just had to be alive to do it.

As he pulled the last of the deer's guts out onto the ground, he thought of his own tiny son, who was next in line to receive the knowledge of men. He washed his hands as best he could in the filthy river. He touched his chest and felt the dog tags beneath his shirt. He prayed that no one would ever have to read them.

Don't Mind the Bunny

On the wall of the hospital gift shop was a stained oak shelf loaded with plush toys, among them a slim yellow bunny with long, ragged ears. Also on the shelf were a lion, a hippo, and a teddy bear. In the course of a day, many men and women passed by the shelf, most looking sad and stressed, some on the verge of tears. One day, a man stood there and quietly spoke of his troubles, to no one in particular.

"My God," he said. "What to get? So much to choose from. If I pick the lion, it might scare her. Most of these are too big; I don't want her to suffocate in her sleep. The bunny looks a little cheap. But somehow…"

He picked up the bunny, ran his fingers up and down its ears. He turned it over and looked at the tail, which was fluffy but small. He must have decided, however, that the bunny was ideal after all, as he walked it to the cash register the next moment.

"Nice," said the woman at the cash register. She scanned the price tag. "This is our most-loved item. Total's $8.99."

"This is your most popular toy?" the man said. "I wouldn't have known just from looking at it." He handed her the money.

"I didn't say it was our most-*purchased* item," she said. "Has the baby been born yet?"

"How did you know?"

She put the bunny in a plastic bag with the receipt and held it out to the man. She smiled. "With the bunny, it's always a birth."

"I see," he said, and he took the bag. "She's with my wife. Thanks for the bunny."

He left the shop and carried the plastic bag with the bunny inside it to the elevator. He went to room 508 and opened the door. Inside was a tired-looking new mother on a hospital bed, nursing an infant girl who had very little hair. The man's face lit up when he saw them. He held up the bag as he walked toward the woman and child.

"Got it," he said.

He handed the bag to the woman, and she put her hand inside and pulled out the bunny. She turned it over a couple of times, examining it.

"This is what you got her?" she said.

"What's wrong with it?"

"It's just a little sad, that's all. Isn't it?"

The man frowned. The woman laughed.

"I'm sorry," she said. "Don't look so dejected. If this is what you chose for her, she's going to love it. It's already growing on me."

She sat the bunny on the bed and reached toward him.

"Come here," she said. She pulled his face into hers and kissed his cheek. "Thank you. For everything."

"It's my job, right?"

He sat in one of the chairs next to her bed and watched as she continued nursing. When the baby girl had had her fill, the woman burped her and then held her up and looked into her eyes, which were barely open. The woman picked up the bunny with her free hand and held it in front of the girl, who almost instantly fell asleep.

Resting on the six-year-old girl's bed was the yellow bunny, now with only one long, ragged ear. The disheveled bedspread was adorned with blue and purple flowers and had yellow-brown stains in some places. A lamp was turned over on the floor, still lit. In the corner of the blue-carpeted room sat the girl, now with a head full of brown hair, quietly drawing on the wall with her feces, her soiled clothes in a pile on the floor. She was laughing when the man came in.

"Jesus Christ!" he said.

He ran to the girl and grabbed hold of both arms. She screamed. She fought to free herself, but the man easily restrained her. She lay down on the floor and repeatedly kicked her feet against the wall, smearing feces on her foot and further soiling the wall and carpet.

"Stop it!" the man said.

She kept screaming and kicking, and it was not long before the woman came into the room and her mouth dropped open. The man looked at her.

"Help me!" he said, trying to hold the girl steady.

The woman rushed over and, taking care to avoid the feces, took hold of the girl's legs while the man held her arms. The girl continued to scream and fight until, finally, she was out of breath and coughing. Her limbs went limp as she coughed, and the man and woman let go. The girl sat up and coughed two more times. Together, the man and woman rubbed her back.

"Are you okay?" the woman said.

The girl seemed not to understand. The man and woman looked at each other and frowned.

"This isn't normal," the man said. "We've ignored it way too long. She's not going to magically get better."

"So what, you think we should call a doctor?"

"What else? We can't keep ignoring the fact that she doesn't really talk. We definitely can't ignore *this*."

He motioned toward the feces on the wall and floor—and on the girl's legs—and then he shook his head.

The woman reached into her pocket and produced a small cellular phone, and then she dialed. She answered questions when prompted. When she had made an appointment, she hung up the phone and put it back in her pocket.

"There's an opening tomorrow at nine," she said. "Someone canceled."

He nodded. She nodded. They looked at the girl, who was silent and was now falling asleep on the floor. Long moments of silence ensued—long, thoughtful moments in which some form of clarity might have come to the man or woman but didn't.

Eventually the woman went to get a bucket of water and some soap, and while she cleaned the floor and walls, the man took care of the girl. When they were finished, they lay there until morning, the three of them snoring quietly on the clean bedroom floor.

The clock read 8:55 a.m. when the man, woman, child, and bunny entered the waiting room at the doctor's office. They sat down in chairs along the wall, with the girl in the middle. She made the bunny hop up and down on her lap. She smiled and then held the bunny to her chest.

To the girl's left sat the woman, reading a magazine, flipping back and forth through the pages. To the girl's right, the man sat and bounced his feet. The girl did not seem to notice anything but the bunny on her lap, with its sewn hole at the top where the ear had gone missing. She ran her finger along the stitches.

It was some time before a female nurse came out and called the girl's name. When she did, the man and woman stood up and helped the girl out of her chair. She held on tight to the bunny, and as they crossed the threshold into the office area, the clock read 9:07 a.m.

"I'm sorry to keep you waiting," the doctor said when they were finally in his office. "Were you here long?"

"Not very," the man said.

"Good," the doctor said, and he smiled. "Now then, what's your name, little girl?"

The girl said nothing. In fact, she acted as if she had also heard nothing.

"That's why we're here," the man said, "among other things. First thing, she's six years old, and she doesn't really speak. Come to think of it, I don't think I've ever once—"

"Our daughter's never said an intelligible word," the woman said. She closed her lips tightly.

"I'm sorry to hear that," the doctor said. "What else?"

The woman cleared her throat. "She smeared shit on her bedroom wall last night. Isn't that a sign of autism?" Tears welled in her eyes but did not spill.

The man glanced at the woman and then looked at the doctor. "What do you think it is, doctor?" he said. "What can we do?"

"I can refer you to a specialist," the doctor said. "This is a behavior issue, which could be linked to any number of developmental concerns. Autism is just one. A specialist can run tests to figure it out. Just to warn you, there's a long road ahead. A lot of progress has been made in the field, though. I'm optimistic you and your child will reap the benefits."

From her chair between the man and woman, the girl sat quietly, hopping the bunny up and down on her lap. She seemed unaware that anything was being said, let alone that she herself was the subject of conversation.

One night, the yellow bunny sat on the dinner table next to the girl, who was now seven years old. It had no ears. It rested among the salt and pepper shakers and the dishes of carrots and potatoes and pot roast and carrot cake. Although the bunny had faded in color, and the carrots were bright orange and therefore noticeable, it was the most regal object on the table. It commanded attention.

"Is that thing still there?" the woman said.

She stared at the bunny across the table.

"When might it've left?" the man said. "She loves the thing, it's not going anywhere." He shoveled the last of his food onto his fork and then ate it.

"Do you ever regret buying it?" the woman said. Her plate was already clean.

"No."

The girl silently finished her carrots and reached for the carrot cake. She took a piece in her bare hand and set it on her plate.

"Well, I do," the woman said. "I wish you'd never bought it. Most children outgrow their stuffed animals eventually."

The girl took a large bite of carrot cake, almost too large to fit in her mouth. She looked at the bunny and smiled as she chewed.

"Our daughter isn't most children," the man said.

The woman looked at the girl and then at the bunny. She reached across the table, struggling to grab the bunny, but instead, she knocked it to the floor.

The girl swallowed her cake and looked down.

"Bunny," she said, and she whimpered.

The man and woman looked at her. They paused.

On the floor, the bunny lay facedown. The man went to pick it up, and the woman followed. They each held part of it, gently rubbing the stitches on the top of its head, petting it, a hint of a smile on their lips as if they did not mind that it was there now—and never did.

Fresh

ouise was thirty-two years old and jobless in February 1969, when she found herself moving back into the twelve-room brownstone on Chester Street where she had grown up. She didn't move because she was lonely or because she had been fired from her job or because she had already spent most of her trust fund on rare first editions of French novels, the ones she had been introduced to while in boarding school after her mother's death. Louise moved home mostly because if she didn't, there would be no one left to care for her sick father. She pitied him.

Several times a week, while he lay on the hospital bed that had been installed in his bedroom, staring at the ceiling, she put needles into his bruised, pinpricked arms and flipped a switch. For a moment, she watched as an intricate network of long plastic tubes pumped his blood into an in-home dialysis machine, where the blood was cleaned and then returned to him.

The procedure took about four hours. For several months, they went through it each time in silence. Louise sat in a leather easy chair next to her father and read her books. He stared at the wall opposite him. It was not until July that he spoke during the procedure for the first time.

"What are you reading?" he said.

His voice was soft and weary, but it startled her. Louise pulled her head out of her book to find him looking at the cover. It was a French edition of *The Bride of the Sun* by Gaston Leroux. She wondered how long he had been staring, squinting, trying to read the title without his glasses, which did nothing for his eyesight these days. Even if they did help, she knew he couldn't read French.

"Just an old book from school. You comfortable?"

She had never asked him this before, and now the words felt strange on her lips. Was he comfortable? What a stupid question. She couldn't imagine how he would be, lying there with needles in both arms.

"Mostly," he said. "No less so than yesterday."

"That's good."

She waited for him to say something else.

"Well, I guess it's about that time," she said at last.

She sat the book in the chair and went to turn off the machine. She removed the needles, making sure blood didn't spill everywhere. Her father drifted off while she was finishing her cleanup, so she left him to sleep.

In her room that night, she read more from *The Bride of the Sun*. Though she had read the book in school, she had forgotten most of the plot. She was struck by the notion of sacrificing a female virgin to a sun god. To her, the moon was more feminine and, frankly, more alluring. Which was why, in two days, when astronauts landed on the moon for the first time, she would be watching the whole thing on TV. As Louise began to fall asleep with the book in her arms, she considered what it might look like for a woman to die for the cause of the moon. The last image she saw before she fell asleep was a naked woman anointed with mud, surrounded by men.

The next day was not a dialysis day. Louise spent most of it in her room, finishing *The Bride of the Sun*. But she went out three times to make something for her father to eat—and once more, before bed, to check that he was still alive.

That night in bed, Louise tried to prepare herself mentally for dialysis the following day. Life with her father now was not particularly tiring, but the sight of him on the bed, immobile, with tubes coming out of him, had been off-putting since the day she arrived back home. On the other hand, she was concerned and outraged that the sight of her father like this made her feel anything. When he sent her to school in another country, she learned to live without him. Now she was bothered that any part of her felt like it needed him to be well again. She went to sleep and dreamed he had died.

The next day, Louise went about her daily routine: making breakfast for herself and her father, reading her French novels, and waiting for the time when she would have to hook her father up to a machine to clean his blood. Once the machine was running, she sat down in her easy chair and read for a while, leaving her father to stare at the ceiling. But today, she had a hard time concentrating on the book, and after a while, she set it aside.

"Why did you send me away to France?" she said.

Her father removed his gaze from the ceiling and looked at her. "What makes you ask that?"

"Mom died, and you immediately sent me away. What was I supposed to think?"

"I'd spent all my time working in insurance while your mother raised you," he said. "When she died, I didn't know how to give you a real home on my own. So I sent you to someone who could."

"I didn't see you for four years."

"And I still regret that. I should have visited, at least."

"You didn't speak French. You didn't even learn it afterward."

"I'm sorry, you're right. There's no excuse except that I really thought I was doing the right thing at the time; I know now that it wasn't right. When you left, I cried for a week."

"You never told me that."

"There's a lot I never told you. Do you know how I met your mother?"

Louise shook her head.

"It was raining one night. At the time, your mother drove a 1932 Nash convertible, and those things were a lot longer in the front than they were in the back. They were sort of top-heavy. But anyway, she was driving down close to the river and got stuck in the mud, and I was driving across the bridge and just saw the front of this car sticking up out of the ground. Looked like the earth was swallowing it whole. Then I saw that there was someone, your mother, still inside, and with the rain still coming down and the mud swallowing up the car, she was just filthy. She was covered from head to toe."

He coughed violently, and Louise grabbed a tissue and handed it to him. He coughed again.

"Do you want some water?" she asked.

"No, I'm fine." He cleared his throat. "Where was I?"

"Covered head to toe in mud."

"Right. Well, she was covered, like I said, so I pulled over and ran down there to help her get out. By then, it was too late for the car. I reached for her hand and pulled. She jumped toward the embankment and rammed right into me. Fell right on top of me, and so I was covered now, too. We just sat there on the ground and laughed as her Nash went down in the mud. Eventually it went into the river and got swept away. We never saw it again."

He smacked his lips.

"Maybe I will take some water."

Louise went to the kitchen and filled a glass with water at the sink. Through the window, she could just barely see the moon sitting underneath tree branches. In a matter of hours, if everything went smoothly, U.S. astronauts would be walking on it for the first time. But she was no longer interested in the moon. She went back to her father's room and handed him the glass of water. He drank it. She took the glass and set it on the table next to him.

"Your mother always liked to say I was her hero and I swept her off her feet," he said. "I think it was the other way around. She was stunning, even covered in mud, and—well, you remember: she was a *petite* little thing, and yet she just bowled me over. Well, look at that, I guess I do know a little French. *Petite.* Just don't ask me how to spell it."

Louise laughed. She could see tears in his eyes.

"Thank you," she said. "Thank you for telling me all of this."

"Can we start over? I'd like to get to know my daughter before I die."

"I'd like that."

Louise smiled. She realized she was standing right next to him, holding his hand, and she wondered how long she had been doing so. She checked the clock above her father's bed and found it had been well over four hours since she had turned on the machine; the process was complete. Louise let go of his hand to turn off the machine. She grabbed his hand again.

"*Voilà*," she said with a wink. "Fresh blood."

This time, Louise did not leave her father alone after the session. Instead, she pulled the easy chair closer to him and sat down, and they talked late into the night about the one thing they had in common: the woman who had held them together, who, for fourteen years, had made their house as much of a home as it could be.

King Henry on a Porch Swing

You and the old lady have been bumbling around the home for weeks now in silence, unable to face each other. But one night, she corners you on the porch swing of your subconscious, your comfort place, and bitches at you about sex and Jersey and the day King Henry died, and how dare you ignore her? You want to get up and walk away, but you can't. It's your mind; she's working in your space now.

She speaks—not so much in logical, audible words as in an uncanny barrage of subconscious thoughts and complex concepts and questions, and her patented derision—about the child you didn't want initially. About the way he had sat in his punkin seat, already holding up his own head, confidently, like a great king on his throne, and about the tiny shoes he had been wearing and the ease with which he could nap on the nape of your neck. And most of all, about how careless you had been. Oh, yes, she blames you. She speaks until you can't stand it anymore, until, at last, words fly from your own mouth like balloons finally escaping the wrists of children.

"Shut up, woman! Talking about King Henry on a porch swing won't bring him back."

You wake up, and her side of the bed is empty. The closet door is open, the light is on, and there is nothing inside.

Life on Other Moons

After the war, there was moon dust in their hair and on their faces, and there was moon dust in their lungs. The moonlings carried it with them in pockets—to the Sea of Tranquility and other places on their half of the moon, where there was nothing left after the bombing ended the war and broke the moon in two. The other half of the Sandystone Kingdom dangled there in space, waiting to be reclaimed.

"Father," Alana said, "we have to send a rescue over there. It's been days. There could be survivors."

"With what resources?" the king said. "We have no way to get there, and even if we did, who would go? Me, I suppose?"

"For starters."

The king laughed from somewhere deep inside. It was the laugh not only of a king but also of an old man, a moonling of distinction.

"But if I left, who would lead the people?" he

said. "You, I suppose?"

"Why not?"

"You're too young. It's not protocol."

"But you make the protocol. You're the most powerful moonling alive. Especially now."

Indeed, most of the moon's population had perished in the blast and the fighting that had led up to it, and even Alana's mother, the queen, had disappeared, though no one had managed to find a body in the aftermath.

"You still haven't found her yet, have you?" she said.

He shook his head. "There are other moonlings for me to worry about right now, the ones who are here and starving, barely surviving off the underground supply stores. But I know that our faithful Derek is looking for your mother night and day. If she's out there, he'll find her."

"What if she's stranded and dying on the other side?"

"We both know she can make it on her own until we get to her. Try not to think about it so much."

Alana nodded. With one hand, she gathered her long hair together as if to form a ponytail, and then she let it drape over her shoulder.

"You look so much like her when you do that," the king said. "That hair. It was her defining characteristic, wasn't it?"

"You mean *isn't* it."

"Yes, let's hope."

He tried to smile, and Alana wiped some dust from his shoulder.

"I feel useless," she said. "I'm going to see if I can help anyone."

With that, she left the king to his thoughts. On her way past the Sea of Tranquility, which was now just a dried-up hole, she came upon Derek, and she smiled.

"What news?" she said.

"It's not good, I'm afraid. Still nothing. Either she's dead or she doesn't want to be found."

"I was afraid you'd say that. Guess there's always tomorrow. Walk with me awhile?"

"I could do that."

He offered her his arm, and she took it. They walked in sweeping circles and zigzags through the rubble and the moon dust, toward nowhere, which was all there was. Along the way, they talked at length about recovery and civilization. Then, Derek brought up the topic of the population and how and when to begin rebuilding.

"I think all the men need to be ready," he said. "A day's going to come when we need to be well rested and ready to perform. If I'm telling the truth, I've already been practicing."

He nudged her with his elbow.

"How so?" she said.

"Do you know the Silver sisters?"

"You slept with them?"

"Twice since the bomb went off. Twice each, in fact—and once at the same time."

He laughed, and she pulled her arm away from his.

"I didn't know you'd been giving this so much thought," she said.

"Just sex. Not much to think about."

"I see."

She took a step backward.

"Good day, Derek. I believe Father requires my attention."

She left him there by the sea. When she was far away, she sat down in her loneliness and cried. Her tears spilled into the moon dust and formed a small amount of thick paste in front of her. On each side of her face was a long streak of brown where the salty liquid had merged with dust. She breathed in spurts. The moon dust entered her lungs and made her cough, wildly and at length, until she forgot to cry.

When her emotions settled, she stood up and wiped the tear streaks from her face. She went to find her father, as she had said she would. She found him at the edge, where the other half of the moon should have been. He was not alone. Several women, all with very long hair, had formed a queue nearby, and more were on the way, lining up behind one another.

"What's all this?" she said. "Is everyone just going to will it to come back?" She waved her hand first at the women and then at the other half of the moon.

He turned to face her, a pair of scissors in his hands.

"Nothing that ridiculous," he said. "But you inspired me earlier. I think I have a plan that will work."

"Finally."

"Don't be insubordinate, dear. It's unbecoming of a princess, and you'll be queen one day. You need to set an example."

She hugged him and looked into his eyes. "I didn't mean it. I think it's great you're making plans." She pulled out of the hug. "Really," she said. "Go on. What's the plan? What are the scissors for?"

"We're going to build a bridge."

"A bridge?"

"Yes."

"To the other side of the moon?"

"Yes."

Alana thought for a moment. "But there's nothing to build with anymore," she said. "And what are the women here for?"

She looked around. There were mounds of dust as far as the eye could see, much of it rising up and forming a cloud that extended several yards above the surface. Interspersed throughout the dust were pieces of buildings that had once stood as part of the mighty kingdom. And standing among the ruins, waiting, were ten women forming a single-file line.

"Construction has already begun," the king said. "Right now, men are out looking. There's rubble, and we'll use it. Lengths of rope have been found, chunks of concrete can be used, the trusses of ruined bridges, hair. We'll use everything we can get our hands on."

"Did you say hair?" she said.

"Everything." He held up the scissors.

"This is mad."

"Then a mad king I will be. It's the only option we have."

She took a deep breath. She ran her hand through her hair, examining its length.

"I didn't say your hair," the king said.

"Why not? Mine's just as good as anyone else's. Come now, I'll go first. Give me the scissors. I see what they're for now."

He held them to his chest. Alana took a step toward him and pulled the scissors from his grip. With her left hand, she gathered her hair into a ponytail, and as she raised the scissors, the king held his breath.

"It's just hair," Alana said.

She squeezed the handles together, and her ponytail came off in her hand. Then she walked over and handed the scissors to the first woman in line, who cut her own hair off and passed the scissors on. Each woman did the same until the line had depleted.

For several days afterward, men and women continued the search for resources, pulling what little they had from the rubble of their once-glorious kingdom. They brought back the materials piece by piece. Derek was often among this group of scavengers. Alana stayed close to the bridge site in those days to supervise. She did not speak to Derek and did not want to.

When there were enough materials to start building, a team of men and a few women began the process. They started with a base of concrete for strength and, to it, added a glue in the form of paste made from moon dust. The bridge was kept narrow to maximize resources. Blocks of concrete were stacked and glued, extending out from the surface of the moon, toward the other half, and every so often, a piece of wood added more length. The rope and hair provided much of the flooring.

Throughout the first nine weeks of construction, Derek was often in the company of women nearby, hardly working, sometimes disappearing with them. So it was not much of a surprise to anyone when, in the span of a few days, three women revealed they were with child.

The first time, the reaction had been neutral from most of the moonlings. The king himself had even congratulated the woman. When the second woman came forward a few days later, however, the king was not pleased, though he directed his frustration only at Derek.

"We barely have enough food as it is!" he said, spraying a constellation of spit onto the ground. "What will we do with another mouth to feed, boy? What were you thinking?"

Derek frowned. "I wasn't, but is it so bad?" he said. "Moonlings'll die out if we don't do something soon."

"We can't know that yet. There could be a whole colony on the other side of this bridge. Our supplies are dwindling, and if it comes down to it, you will be the one to go without."

With this declaration, the king left, and the moonlings continued to build. Even Derek kept working, though now he appeared to be lost in thought. Alana watched him for a while and pitied him. Then she went to join her father for the night.

The next day, when the third woman came forward, cowering, barely able to speak the words, the king was enraged. He declared that until the bridge was complete—likely later that day— women should not go near the construction site. Alana was the one exception. He looked around at the women, raising his eyebrows, and they began to leave the site.

"And as for you," he said, pointing at Derek, "there's only one option. You created life we can't possibly support. You were careless, and there's no excuse. So I can't allow you to go on."

"What's that mean?" Derek said.

"I think you know."

The king raised his hand. The two men who stood closest to Derek grabbed hold of his arms. He breathed in and then out, and a small puff of dust formed in front of him.

"Is this the only way?" he asked.

"It is."

Derek bowed his head for a moment and then looked at the king. "Then I have to accept it," he said. "I'm sorry, if it's worth anything."

"It's not."

The king turned to give Alana a quick nod before storming off. Then Alana looked at Derek and found he was already watching her. Their eyes met as a dust cloud passed through the space between them. She reached out to touch his chest, and the men tightened their grip on his arms.

"What have you done?" she said.

"I didn't plan it, that's for sure."

"If you had, you might've told me, and I would've slapped some sense into you. You've put us all in danger. And you've hurt me more than any war ever did."

"I didn't know."

"You didn't *think!*" She shoved him with the heel of her hand and then backed away. "You never do, and it makes me crazy."

"I didn't know you gave me that much thought," he said.

"I guess now there's not much to think about. Or maybe there's too much, I can't decide."

And with that, Alana left him, once more going off in search of her father. She found him sitting by the sea and gazing out at its vast emptiness. She approached from behind. He spoke before she had even reached him.

"You probably would have done things differently. She would have, too."

"Maybe a little."

She put her head on his shoulder.

"Your mother was always better at this than me," he said. "The punishments, the planning, any amount of public speaking. She was fiercer and more cunning than I'll ever be. She was a better leader, and she would have had this moon back together by now."

"But she's not here. You are."

"This is true, unfortunately. Where is she when I need her?"

Alana lifted her head. They faced each other.

"I miss her, too," Alana said, "but she's strong. Like you said, if she's alive, we'll find her. Derek will help us. Speaking of Derek, what're we going to do about him and his children? You certainly can't mean to kill him for this. He's been with us for so long."

"You love him."

It was a statement, but it was also a question, and it was one that Alana had never faced directly. She considered her answer.

"If I'm being honest, I'm not sure what I feel now. He can be such an idiot, but I did care for him and maybe still do. Can you spare him? Can we find another way?"

"I know I overreacted. Your love is safe. But there can't be any more accidents. Clearly, I wouldn't know how to handle them."

He smiled, and she kissed his cheek. They sat together on the edge of the sea for a while and then made their way back to the bridge, which now appeared to be complete. He called all the women back to the bridge, and the men began to gather around as well.

"As you may know," the king said when everyone had gathered around him, "certain circumstances have forced me into an embarrassing rage. I'm sorry for acting so harshly in front of you all. Derek, we'll solve this problem rationally. There's no sense killing anyone at a time like this."

Alana's eyes met Derek's. A feeble smile approached his lips.

"But be warned," the king said. "No more. We have all the moonlings we can sustain until we know what lies on the other side."

He looked at the other half of the moon and

then at the bridge. Two men were walking across it, toward them.

"What news?" the king said when they were back on the safety of the moon's surface.

"It's done," one of them said. "We can cross."

The king reached for Alana's hand and squeezed. She looked at him and then at Derek and then at the other moonlings.

"It's time," the king said. "Soon, we'll know if there's life on the other side. And if there's only death, we'll face it with dignity and courage. And we'll rebuild."

He let go of Alana's hand and then pointed at the bridge.

"After you, dear," he said.

Alana went to the bridge and put one hand on each concrete side. She looked back at Derek as she stepped onto the floor made of rope and hair, and as she turned to face the bridge once more, she coughed, and a small cloud of dust rose up above her. And one by one, with hope in their hearts, the moonlings followed her to the other side of the moon, where they would search for life amid the death they had endured.

Looking

Every evening, the waves come rushing back into the streets like a herd of Spanish bulls, and everyone scatters. They run up High Hill and stand at the top. Mostly, they wonder if the water will reach them this time. Fear is a tradition and a fact of life in this town—where the sea routinely runs in herds, washing away everything not anchored down, and even fishermen are somewhat uneasy about water.

The town's inhabitants are creatures of habit. They eat breakfast at dawn every day, sitting on blankets at the beach. They look out over the sea. They fish until noon and then lay sandbags in town for as long as they can. Their homes are mostly protected when the tide brings the water around six o'clock, or five if the moon is feeling especially vindictive, and the people run to higher ground.

The girl who can't speak is always among the people on High Hill. She is a teenage orphan, generally ignored during the day. She lost her family in waves. Nonetheless, she welcomes the waves, now, and the chance to evade them by climbing High Hill. That's when everyone is together, looking at one another, performing head counts. She needs everyone to be looking from time to time. As if she matters, too.

When the waters recede, she waits to leave High Hill until the last possible second. Finally, the men say, "Let's go now," and the women say, "Come on, let's get some peace." She has no choice but to go. They have the power of speech. Who is she to deny them?

At the center of town is a sandbag shack, and that's where she goes each night out of habit—and the men follow, and the women stop looking when the door is shut, and she is no longer ignored. Inside, she thinks about control. Is there a way to say no without actually saying it? In the sandbag shack, she might get an hour of sleep if the men get tired soon enough. When she emerges in the morning, no one speaks. The men come out behind her, one by one, and the women look the other way. Everyone begins the day looking.

They eat breakfast on blankets at the beach, looking out over the sea. They fish and look at the sea. When it's time to sandbag their homes for protection, they do so with one eye on the sea. In the evening, the waters come running. Everyone is ready.

She is ready most of all. She stands on top of High Hill, looking out, and it might as well be a mountaintop. She is safe there. She is accounted for. When the tide recedes, she yearns to leave High Hill last or not at all. But she always leaves.

Love the Shoes

arvey Brogan sat on the best stretch of pale yellow grass The Gate had to offer, knees bent, feet flat on the ground. His eyes were transfixed on the prison-issued tennis shoes he'd worn for several years now, taking them in one last time. He admired their comfortable insoles but cursed the thinness of their throats and the shoddy stitching of their welts. Today, he would be released with the shoes he'd had on when he was brought to The Gate, that old model whose soles were a mustard yellow and whose uppers were all black with a hint of red, and then he would be off to see his fourteen-year-old son, Kendrick, for the first time in many years. For that occasion, he was going to need a newer model.

He'd had three pairs of cheap tennis shoes during his nine years at The Gate. All were originally white nylon low-tops with beige shoelaces and a cream tongue that carried his last name in permanent black marker. In the outside world, he'd always avoided white shoes. Over the years, they tended to take on the color of everything the wearer touched, even the grass on which he walked. By now, his no-brand shoes had lost some of their initial luster, though he'd done all he could to keep them pristine. For nine years, with every pair of shoes he wore, he walked slowly. He took careful steps to avoid scuffing. Some days, just for an hour or so, he pulled off the shoes and went around his cell with naked toes to give his no-brand walking shoes a break. On Sundays, he didn't even wear shoes.

But today was a Friday, and he was being released from prison. As he watched the guard come to retrieve him from atop the hill, he tried to imagine what his son might look like now and what he might wear. Harvey pictured a younger version of himself: blond hair, gray eyes with specks of brown, maybe tall for his age, wearing dark-colored low-tops with dark welts and dark toe caps to conceal dirt from walking. When Harvey last saw Kendrick, the boy was naked from the ankle down, so this would be a step up. If nothing else, Harvey could soon check to see that Kendrick's arch had developed properly; otherwise Kendrick might need something with a custom waist for better support. In any good relationship with shoes, support was key. Running or walking;

Velcroed or laced; black, white, or brightly colored—none of this mattered if the waist had no support. But Harvey hoped for the best. He wanted Kendrick to have options. Kendrick would be a young man now, after all, with preferences all his own.

The guard reached the top of the hill. He tried to smile, but it looked more like he was baring his teeth to show authority. Harvey wondered if the guard was ever afraid of The Gate. If so, he didn't blame him. The Gate was a scary place if one didn't have his wits about him. Something, or someone, might come at him out of the blue. He stood up, and they started down the hill.

"I bet your wife is thrilled you're coming home," the guard said as they walked.

And there it was, right out of nowhere. This guard was friendly but new, and he clearly hadn't heard: Harvey's wife had recently passed away. Having already lost her nine years prior, Harvey hadn't needed much time to adjust. He'd made peace with it. Still, he considered what Kendrick might be going through—losing one parent and gaining another he barely knew. What would Harvey say to the boy when they met? He decided he would not bring up the boy's mother.

"Thanks," he said. "I'm going to see my son today. Have to get some new shoes first, though."

"Oh yeah? How old?"

"He's fourteen. The shoes are ten, if that's what you meant."

"It wasn't. You nervous?"

"Terrified."

"You just need to get him talking about something, that's all. Ask him about girls." He winked. "See you later. Or maybe I won't, eh? Have a great life. Or have a life, anyway."

The guard touched Harvey's shoulder and then walked away. Harvey stood at the counter and waited for the checkout proceedings to begin.

Kendrick had just arrived from his uncle's house, where he had been staying since his mom died, and gone straight to his bedroom. Harvey stood in the doorway and looked in. He noticed that Kendrick wore black Converse high-tops with what appeared to be nail polish graffiti all over the canvas material constituting the uppers. His clothes were all black. His hair was dyed black as well, and it was spiked so high that it seemed to stand a good six inches taller than Harvey.

Kendrick himself was a mountain. Harvey remembered the growth chart they'd started on the kitchen wall. He wondered if it was still there and how high it had reached. Just under six feet, he guessed. He would look at it later to confirm.

"It's great to meet you, son," Harvey said, his voice unexpectedly soft. He imagined himself as a small butterfly struggling to make himself heard. He cleared his throat.

"I guess."

Kendrick's voice was deep, which would have surprised Harvey if the boy hadn't already been so tall. Harvey motioned toward the bed. They sat down.

"Love the shoes," Harvey said. "What size?"

"Eleven."

"Already? You'll be bigger than me before long."

Kendrick took off one of his shoes and started picking at the brown rubber outsole where a large chunk was missing. It appeared to have been dug out with a knife, and Kendrick was peeling pieces away, making the hole wider and deeper.

"It's in our genes," Harvey said.

"What is?"

"Shoes. We come from a long line of shoemakers. It's what our name means. Brogan."

"Lucky me. Another embarrassing family fact the school doesn't need to know."

Harvey shrugged. "How is school? Get any decent grades? I know I didn't."

Kendrick threw a particularly large chunk of rubber on the floor.

"What about friends?" Harvey said. "Any good ones I should know about?"

"Good ones? What exactly are you asking me, Harvey?" Kendrick looked up and stared accusingly into Harvey's eyes. He didn't wait for a response, though, before looking back down and digging more rubber out of his shoe.

"I'm sorry. I just want to know you. I want to know who you hang out with, where you like to go, what kinds of shoes you like to wear." Harvey's hand felt heavy as he reached out to touch Kendrick's shoulder. "If there's someone you love, maybe."

Kendrick stopped digging at the shoe to shrug Harvey's hand away.

"No, no one," he said without looking up.

Harvey watched Kendrick continue to dig pieces out of his shoe's outsole and throw them on the floor as they came free. There wasn't much there to begin with, though. He'd forgotten this about Converse shoes. The sole consisted mostly of one flat piece of rubber that provided little or no comfort.

"I bet these things are hell on your gait cycle," he said.

Was he allowed to say *hell* to a fourteen-year-old? He couldn't remember.

"I don't know what that means," Kendrick said. He looked at Harvey.

"Your gait is the way you move. As long as you have legs that aren't damaged in any way and you've been taught how to use them, you have both a walking gait and a running gait. Everyone walks and runs differently, of course. The gait cycle is all about the progression from one gait to another. You can move through them as easily as putting your foot in a shoe. And some shoes are best for running. Because of the way your foot lands. When you run, you're all the way up in the air for a second, so you need more support for when you come back down. When you walk, you just put one foot in front of the other. There's less pressure when you walk, so those soles are made differently. You shouldn't really use walking shoes to run, but I guess you could do the opposite and it wouldn't hurt much."

"So what you're saying is, my shoes are good for nothing?"

"I guess so. Especially now." They both looked at the deformed shoe and laughed. Harvey felt better than he had in years. Perhaps he had found his way in. "There's this pair of shoes your mom had—I wonder if they're still in her closet. Anyway, they were made for her, just perfect for her walking gait. They had this beautiful curved breast, which is the front part of the heel—"

"Why do you know so much about shoes?" Kendrick said. He leaned over and took a pocketknife from his bedside table.

"I just do," Harvey said, watching him, curious.

"You know nothing about me but everything about shoes. Even her shoes. It's weird."

Harvey's heart fell. Only hours out of The Gate, and he'd already broken his promise not to talk about the boy's mother. He watched Kendrick stab the shoe's outsole and start cutting off a new piece to throw on the floor.

"I know that when I was taken away, she had twenty-seven pairs of high heels, six pairs of tennis shoes, ten pairs of sandals, and two pairs of boots, and I loved her. I know that when you were little, you liked to walk around without shoes like an Amish kid with feet as tough as steel. And I loved you, too."

"All you know is shoes."

"Maybe. But there's a lot of good stuff to know about shoes. I can fix that one, for example. Go ahead. Cut the hole damn sole off, and I can fix it. Sorry, I said damn."

Kendrick put down the knife and smiled.

"I'm fourteen," he said. "I've heard it. I've said it."

"Good. Well, not good, obviously—you shouldn't say that." He started to give Kendrick a stern finger in the face but thought better of it. "Anyway, just put some rubber and a skiver and some glue in front of me, maybe a needle and thread with some material to create a new welt, and I can fix any sole. I can make it better than ever, in fact. Your gait will thank me."

Kendrick put down the shoe.

"It's just a shoe, though," he said. "What about the other stuff? You were gone…"

Harvey nodded, frowning. "Nine years. I thought about you every day I was in The Gate."

"That's really what it was called?"

"That's what they called it."

Kendrick clicked his tongue a couple of times.

"I bet you didn't think about me every day," he said. "You couldn't have. That's a lot of days."

"Every day. In my head, you even had a pair of shoes for every day and every gait in your cycle. I could list them."

Kendrick thought for a moment. He put his hands on his knees and rubbed them up and down. Then he stopped moving, his hands resting on his lap. "What were you in for?"

"Theft," Harvey said. "Of shoes."

Kendrick laughed for several seconds, probably longer than he meant to. But he didn't ask for the truth.

Harvey reached out and put his hand on his son's shoulder. This time, Kendrick let him. Harvey smiled. Life on the outside was far from perfect, but he was home again, and he was a father again. It was a gait he could get used to.

Home on the Moon

The year 1972 is coming to a close, which means rain and darkness all the time in Vietnam, and you're stationed next to the river. So it rains, and you're up to your knees in the black, slimy floodwaters of the Song Tra Bong. The dead boy lies there along the banks. He floats in the vast overflow like something being carried away by ants. His eyes are open, pelted with never-ending drops from the sky. You wonder how he can keep them open like that, and then you remember: he's dead. You remember how you had to shoot his ear off to stop him and how he had kept running toward you with his rifle and you had to shoot him in the forehead. Filthy, red-black blood oozes from the wound, dripping down into the slime.

And everything is putrid. You're dressed like a tree—the better to stay hidden—and you smell like a toilet because everything does. It's the Song Tra Bong.

But the worst part is how young he is. The boy you killed reminds you of your son, who you don't even know anymore, who was six years old when you left him. The dead boy and your son are about twelve. You look at the body they seem to share now and see the last bit of innocence being swallowed up by war. A boy who hasn't begun to shave yet, who's probably never kissed a girl. A boy with dirt on his face, playing soldier like children do. Idolizing the protectors of his country.

The boy lies there in shadow, and all you can see is your son, who waits patiently on the porch swing at the edge of your mind. As if he just wants to talk. The moon shines through the clouds for the first time in weeks, illuminating the dead boy's face, and you see it, and he really does look like he could be him: your son, who liked to build things, back when you knew him, and maybe still does. You wish you knew him now, what he really looks like. You wish he could build you and him and Calpurnia a home far away—perhaps on the moon itself, in a dusty oasis far from the cesspool of Vietnam—and you could get to know him again.

Most of all, you wish the moon wasn't so powerful at night. In Vietnam, the dark is pitch-black, so any amount of moonlight is like a beam from the sun. In Vietnam, the moon is complicit in your actions because it shows them to you. The boy you had to kill is only about twelve. It's all there in his lit-up face; you just have to look. So you do, and you wonder how this could happen so soon. He's twelve. Why did no one ever talk him out of this? He lies there, sinking, being swallowed up in the valley of the Song Tra Bong. As the last of him disappears under the slime, you gaze into the face of your son—a future painter, maybe, or an architect, but a visionary in any case—and for just a few seconds, you are proud, and you are at home on the moon.

The Paper Man

We lived among the coconut trees near the shore, and since our meat supply had become so scarce lately, we looked to the coconut for sustenance. It was adequate; it was versatile. Raw, fire-grilled, toasted, roasted, blackened, charred—the taste we required could be controlled with a little forethought as to how long the coconut was on the fire. Still, the meat of it was really just fruit. We hadn't seen a boar or even a squirrel in weeks, and our taste buds were eager for something more complex and wild. There was a fear in our group that we might never have real meat again. Then the man came.

It was Areka who spotted him first and recognized him for what he was. The distinct masculine curve of his jaw, the broadness of his shoulders, the long, distinguished black beard: this creature was indeed a man. And we would know. All our lives, we'd gathered around campfires late at night to hear descriptions of men from the women old enough to remember them. But there was something in the man's appearance that was surprising even to the elder ladies. Where the man should have worn layers of mud, like us, to shield himself from the sun while allowing movement, he wore a light papery substance instead. It covered up his manly form and, no doubt, made it difficult to move, for fear of tearing.

Near a large oak tree, he set about gathering acorns one at a time with his nose, inching them forward, rolling them into three equal piles. He was careful not to tear the paper as he crawled. He worked slowly. We could see that the man was primitive.

As we watched him work, we slathered new layers of mud on our bare breasts, rubbing outward from the nipple, and then eventually covered our shoulders and faces. When we were dressed, we took up our bows and charged forth.

At the oak, we surrounded him. He froze. His eyes shifted from breast to breast, opened up wide, as if he'd never seen a woman before. We, too, hesitated for a moment, drinking in the sight of a man who, for all we knew, was made mostly of paper. We threw aside our bows and moved close enough to touch him. He blinked, and Areka grabbed hold.

When she tightened her grip on him, the brute cried out, and we heard a fear that went unrivaled in the annals of our history. There was a pathetic, raspy quality to the man's voice, a cracking, as if he himself were about to break into a thousand useless scraps and fall down on us.

"Primitives," Areka said in disgust, and we all seized him.

With somewhat of a struggle, we dragged him away from the oak, drawing lines in the earth with his legs. He screamed until he was hoarse. Then he just cried.

Back at our camp, Areka restrained him while we stoked the fire and prepared the apparatus that would hold him in place above it. He would burn up nicely, with all that paper, and we were eager to eat him when he charred. His paper would turn to ash and float above us, raining into our hair as we enjoyed his body.

Meanwhile, Areka sat on his chest. She held his hands against the ground, and when he struggled, his paper suit began to tear. So he stopped moving; he stopped crying; he hardly even sniffled. Eventually, Areka let go of his hands, and we stopped to watch them.

Areka looked at his mouth, touched his lips, tidied his wild beard with her fingertips. He gave a slight smile. Then their eyes met, and she inched forward. He was gentle, still. Harmless.

"Sisters," she said, and she looked up to face us. "We are starved for meat—this is true—but how can we eat this man when he's the first we've seen? I think there's something here we might need more than sustenance. Look in his eyes. There is something wonderful there."

She looked down again, and we followed suit. There was indeed something there, but whatever it was, it existed beyond us entirely.

"Is this what the elder ladies call—do you think this is love, sisters?" The elders were napping, so we had no one to ask. We were silent.

As the fire raged behind us, we regarded his gentle eyes, his paper covering, his beard. His manliness. And our appetites rumbled. For the first time, though, we didn't quite know what it was that we hungered for. It wasn't a simple thing like food. Instead, there was something in the man's eyes that said "home" to us in a way that we had never encountered. We had the last man in our clutches, and although we had never even seen one before, we knew that he was what we needed to carry on as a people.

Walking to Vietnam

In September 1968, a family in rural Alabama was preparing for war. Soon the father would be shipped overseas to wear a uniform and save the world while sleeping under the moon and the stars, and the mother and son would be left behind to carry on, proud but alone. The concerns of each family member at this time were quite different.

Victor, the father, had a particular stake in the safety of his interracial family. There had been whispers in the town when he had married Calpurnia, but so far, they had never become threatening. Now he would be leaving the country, and God only knew when he would return. Meanwhile, Calpurnia worried about heartbreak and what the lack of a constant man would do to their son's development. Six-year-old Jacob was often in another world entirely, concerned with the intricacies of his own imagination. He was a builder, a dreamer, and with each new world he created for himself, the distractions involved would become a potential coping mechanism. Indeed, Victor believed his son would be okay, that Jacob's concerns would be relegated to the superpowers he might have on the moon or the science of teleportation, not the number of years spent without a father. Calpurnia was unconvinced.

The day before Victor was to deploy, young Jacob was playing by the creek after school. On the adjacent bank, he saw a black dog sprinting toward him, panting heavily. It jumped in the water and swam across, and when it reached him, he put his hand out to pet it.

"I'll keep you," he said, and the dog licked his face.

Jacob laughed and fell to the ground. He wrapped his arms around the dog's neck and squeezed, and he breathed in the cold smell of wet dog. Feeling it struggle against his hug, he released it. The dog scratched at a bald spot on its ear. Jacob expected it to run off, so he watched it carefully. No dog would escape him without a fight. He grabbed it by the collar and pulled it around the yard, looking for some way to contain it. He found a rope next to the garage. He tied the dog to a nearby tree, using one of the knots his father had taught him the previous summer.

That night after dinner, when Victor and Calpurnia caught their son trying to feed the dog table scraps, there was a difference of opinion. They stood outside by the tree where the dog was tied, and they argued. Jacob, of course, saw the utmost value in the dog, while his mother was adamant: it had to go.

"I don't see what's so wrong with him having a dog," Victor said, joining Jacob's side, although he was thinking more about Calpurnia's protection than anything else.

"No," Calpurnia said. "You won't have to clean up the crap. You know that job would just fall to me, and I won't do it. Besides, look at him scratch; this dog's got fleas."

Victor sighed. She had him. He was leaving the next day and did not know when he would be back; no one did.

"Okay," he said. "You're right."

"But dad!" Jacob said.

"No, you get rid of it. Untie him right now and let him run off. Don't you try to bring him back, either. No tricks."

Jacob untied the dog and shooed it away. The dog hesitated, lifted a paw as if to shake. But Jacob turned his back until, finally, the dog ran into the woods. Jacob threw the rope on the ground. He ran to the house, through the door, and up the stairs to his room. He cried into his pillow that night. Occasionally he heard the faint clatter of objects colliding or doors opening and then closing as Victor and Calpurnia went about the home and made their final preparations for war.

When Victor knocked on Jacob's door for a goodbye the next morning, Jacob did not answer. Victor opened the door and walked up to Jacob's bed. He looked at his son, and though he felt the boy's pain, he knew that Calpurnia's instinct had been right. Jacob could not have a dog. He was simply too young for that kind of responsibility, at least with only one parent around to help out.

"I'm leaving now. Going to a place called Vietnam. Do you know where that is?"

Jacob looked at the ceiling.

"It's clear on the other side of the world. Look, I know you're mad at me, but your mom's right. A dog is too much to handle right now."

He waited again for Jacob to respond.

"I'm leaving, son, and I don't know when I'll be back. I'm a little scared. Say goodbye to me."

Jacob remained silent. After a minute, Victor relented and said goodbye once more. He touched Jacob's hair, brushed it with his fingers, and left the room.

When Calpurnia came to Jacob's room a few minutes later, her lips closed tight, he turned on his side. She closed the door and walked away as his tears once again seeped into the pillow.

On the last day of school the following spring, Calpurnia sat in her car at the front of the parking lot, engine off, waiting for Jacob to come out of the building. Just as the bell rang and students started pouring out, a woman knocked on Calpurnia's window. She was pale and wore dark sunglasses with small diamonds on either side.

"Excuse me," she said when Calpurnia rolled down the window. "You're in my spot."

"Am I? I didn't see your name on it."

The woman pushed her sunglasses up so they sat neatly on her head. She put her hand on the top of Calpurnia's car and leaned forward a few inches.

"Don't be a bitch."

Calpurnia looked at the swarm of kids coming toward the parking lot. Among them, near the front, was Jacob. She looked at the woman.

"It's no one's spot, lady. Ain't nobody can't park anywhere she damn well pleases. This is a public school, that's how it works."

"For some people, maybe."

"For all people," Calpurnia said. She started the car. "Look, my son's coming now. If you take your hand off my car and step back, I'll be on my way."

The woman smiled. She leaned forward several more inches, and then she spat on Calpurnia's face. She removed her hand from the car and walked away.

Calpurnia wiped her face on her sleeve and then looked up to see Jacob standing in front of the car with wide eyes. He got inside. He put his backpack on the floor.

"Mommy, what happened?"

"Nothing much. Just a little disagreement, that's all."

"That woman spitted on you."

"And that's all it was, baby, don't you worry about it none."

They drove home in silence. In the driveway, Calpurnia parked the car and turned off the engine. Jacob left his backpack on the car floor as usual and ran inside, straight to the refrigerator. He pulled out two wrapped deli packages, one containing cheese and the other containing bologna. He grabbed the loaf of bread from the counter and moved everything to the table, where he made his afternoon sandwich. He took his first bite just as Calpurnia walked in with his backpack.

"I don't know how you can eat that stuff," she said. "Just the smell makes me sick." She wrinkled her nose.

"It's yummy."

"If you say so. You like it, that's all that matters."

"Daddy likes bologna too."

She laughed. "I never pretended he was perfect." She put the backpack on the floor and kissed his hair. "I'm going to take a quick shower. Don't open the front door for nobody."

She walked away, and Jacob took another bite of his sandwich. While he ate, he thought about the woman from that afternoon. Calpurnia had said there was a disagreement, but Jacob remembered other times when he had seen women get that close to her. Until this day, however, he had never seen one of them spit in her face. This image struck him. The woman was very upset, and Jacob could not think of one thing Calpurnia could have done to make her so.

He was thinking about this, trying to come up with a reason, when he heard a knock on the door. He finished his sandwich in one bite and went to see who was there. It was the woman. Jacob remembered that Calpurnia had told him not to let anyone in, but how else was he going to get answers? He opened the door.

The woman stood on the front porch, wearing her sunglasses, which she moved to the top of her head when she saw Jacob. She shifted her weight to one side.

"Hello there," she said. "Is your—I guess is your maid home?"

Jacob looked around.

"Mam, I don't think we have a maid."

"You're a polite little thing, aren't you?" She pinched his chin and then sighed. "I must have followed the wrong car."

"Are you here to see my mommy?"

"I sincerely doubt it."

"You spitted on her today. Didn't you come to say sorry?"

The woman looked confused. She shifted her weight to her other leg.

"That black woman is your mother?" she said. "You look so…normal."

The bathroom door opened. Jacob turned around as Calpurnia came into the living room in a robe, drying her hair with a towel.

"I told you not to answer that door," she said. "Who is it?"

She reached the door before he could answer. She threw the towel on the living room floor and put both arms out, grabbing each side of the doorway. She stared hard at the woman.

"Jacob, leave us. I told you not to answer this door."

Jacob sat on the couch and folded his hands in his lap.

"What do you want?" Calpurnia said to the woman.

"I'm really not sure anymore. I wasn't expecting to see a kid."

"I told you I was picking up my son. Why else would I be at that school?"

"I mean a real kid. I mean I wasn't expecting him to be so—God, he's almost white."

"What of it? His daddy's all white. You got no right to judge us, but that sure don't stop you. Let's get one thing clear, though: don't you ever touch my son. Ever."

"I wouldn't dream of it," the woman said. "He's not the enemy."

"Wake up, lady. The only enemy out there right now is this fool war. You go to Vietnam, where my husband is, and then you come back and tell me there's something wrong with my family."

"Just stay to the back of the parking lot next year, where you belong, and we won't have anything more to talk about. Have a nice summer."

And with that, the woman pushed her sunglasses back down to her eyes and walked off. Calpurnia watched the woman get into her car and drive away. Then she slammed the door shut and spun on Jacob, who was still sitting on the couch. She pointed her finger at him.

"I told you not to open that damn door for no one!"

"I'm sorry, Mommy, I thought she came to say sorry."

"You thought wrong."

She relaxed her hand at her side, and Jacob looked at it, really saw it. While the back of her hand was dark, almost black, her palm and fingernails were noticeably paler. But still nothing like his. He looked at his own hands. He looked up.

"Why do you and me have different colors of skin?" he said.

Calpurnia sat down.

"It's just how we were born," she said. "Some people have darker skin than others."

"I know, but I mean why am I like Daddy and not you?"

"You just are, Jacob. I guess I don't know why. I'm not science-smart. Maybe you'll understand one day and you'll explain it to me."

Without another word, Calpurnia left Jacob alone on the couch. He tried to make sense of what he had learned but found he could not. He needed to know more. What he really needed was to talk to his father, and that was just what he was going to do, even if he had to walk all the way to Vietnam to find him. But Jacob did not really know where Vietnam was.

He went to the back door and stepped outside. By now, the sun was setting, and a broken moon had risen in the sky. He looked at it. A whole chunk was missing on one side as if someone had taken a bite out of it. Jacob had seen this happen before, always assuming the other part was just hidden somehow, but it had never had much meaning. This time was different. He needed to be somewhere else, and looking up at half a moon, realizing that the other half must be somewhere, he knew that the same was true of his father. Somewhere on the other side of the world, perhaps hidden in shadow, was his father, fighting a war to save the world.

Jacob ran down the hill toward the creek, but he stopped at the edge of the water. He had never been allowed to cross it without an adult around. An adult like his father, whom he desperately needed to see. Jacob considered any punishment he might receive and decided it would be worth it if it meant he could see his father. He plowed through the cold creek, and when he reached the opposite bank, he felt movement as something walked up on the left. He turned. It was a dog. Jacob could not tell if it was the same dog as the one he had had to turn away, but right now, it did not matter. All that mattered was finding Vietnam. He ran into the woods, and the dog followed.

As he ran, he wondered what Vietnam might look and sound like and whether the people there had light or dark skin, and he thought about the cruel, evil nature they would surely have and the size of Vietnam and how far across the land he would have to go, once he was there, to find his father. Although he had no answers for his questions, the more he thought about them, the clearer things became. He could hear gunfire to his right and bombs to his left, and he ran through a blanket of darkness in a thicket of nearly invisible trees. There was no sun, no moon, no light whatsoever, but still, when enemy fire rumbled through the air nearby, he crouched to avoid being spotted. He could not see the enemy. Either it was too dark to see them or they were too dark to see. The noise of gunfire stopped. He started running again and felt the dog's hot breath on his heels. He ran for what felt like hours, dropping to the ground whenever he heard gunfire, and his side was beginning to hurt from the running when he saw light up ahead. He laughed, and the pain of it made him wheeze. When he finally broke through the darkness, he stepped into a moonlit street. On a road sign was the first big word he had learned to spell: *Alabama*. His father was still half a world away.

Jacob returned home that night with the dog's guidance. He walked. He was no longer in a hurry. When they arrived at the creek, he turned to face the dog and then rubbed the top of its head.

"I can't keep you," he said. "Go."

He spun around to face the water. Leaving the dog behind, he crossed the creek and walked up to the house he had lived in his entire life. Quietly, he opened the door and went inside, and he wondered if this would be his house forever. It did not feel much like home without his father. Jacob missed him now more than ever. He crept upstairs to his room and went to sleep.

When he woke, Calpurnia was sitting at the foot of his bed, frowning. "Don't you ever leave this house without telling me," she said. "Ever."

For several weeks after that, Jacob squandered his vacation. He spent most of the summer of 1969 in his bedroom. Other kids his age who had fathers in Vietnam had managed to carry on swimming, fishing, camping out, having sleepovers, playing baseball, and planning elaborate heists to sneak ice cream before dinner. But Jacob resigned himself to staring at the ceiling. He counted shadows and compared their darkness to the light tones of everything else. He took controlled breaths and counted them. Some days, if he felt up to a challenge, he tried to draw pictures of Vietnam and war and his father, but each time, he failed to make even a single pencil stroke. There was no imagination left.

Meanwhile, having noticed a change in Jacob, Calpurnia kept a close eye on him in the weeks after school ended. She made a point to ask him several times a week if he would like to do something fun—go to a movie, maybe, or eat out someplace he would enjoy even if she did not. But each time, the answer was no.

Calpurnia tried to understand. Jacob was too young to be so moody, and surely he had already forgotten about the woman with the sunglasses. The problem, she decided, must be that Jacob missed his father. In which case she had been right all along: it was not good for a son to be without his father, and this war was dampening the spirits of the whole family, tearing it apart just by existing. Until Victor was home safe, there was no hope of mending. Calpurnia spent her summer waiting for news.

Then, just after 3 p.m. in Alabama on July 20, 1969, or 4 a.m. the next day in Vietnam, the Apollo 11 spacecraft landed on the moon. Jacob and Calpurnia watched the live broadcast in silence from their living room in Alabama, while Victor could only look up at the moon from Vietnam at the appropriate time. In this moment, separated by continents, the family was together in its reverence for the United States. For the first time in history, humans had landed on a celestial body beyond Earth. Nothing else mattered.

When the landing itself was over, Jacob and Calpurnia went about the rest of their day, and Victor tried but failed to sleep. Several hours later, while Victor was out on a mission, the broadcast began again and Jacob and Calpurnia sat down to watch. First, the door of the spacecraft opened. Then, at exactly 9:56 p.m. in Alabama, 10:56 a.m. in Vietnam, the first man set foot on the moon.

For about an hour, Jacob and Calpurnia were silent yet again, mesmerized by the images on the TV. Never before had they witnessed anything so extraordinary. The United States had not only sent people to the moon but had also asked them to walk on it. And Jacob and Calpurnia were able to watch it happen. Somehow the problems they faced seemed small by comparison. There were thousands of U.S. soldiers in Vietnam, and no one knew when they would come home, and Jacob's father was among them—but there were men on the moon.

From the comfort of his own couch, Jacob imagined a simpler life for his family. His father, his mother, and the dog he had longed for were together with him on a rocket blasting toward the moon. Once on the surface, he and his family put on the spacesuits that would allow them to survive. He opened the hatch, and they made their exit. He looked around at the desolate but safe moon. This was where they belonged.

"Welcome home," he said, and together, they bounded off to the Sea of Tranquility.

Gratitude

Thank you so much for reading! Please take a moment to leave a brief review wherever you purchased your copy of the book. If you have a Goodreads account, it would be great if you could post your review there, too.

About the Author

Roger Market is originally from Montezuma, Indiana. He graduated from Wabash College in 2009 with a BA in English and a minor in history. He received his MFA in Creative Writing & Publishing Arts in 2013 from the University of Baltimore, and this book is the result of that study. As of the time this edition was published, you can find him on the web at www.roger.market.

About the Design

This book was designed and typeset entirely by its author, Roger Market, in Adobe InDesign. Its main typeface is Adobe Caslon Pro, and there is one glyph set in Minion Pro. The title page and all headings and other sundries are set in Futura. The author also enjoys Optima, Gill Sans, and Adobe Garamond Pro. Fellow MFA student Danielle Crawford graciously provided the author photo, which the author processed and placed on the back cover.